For Dear Wei[illegible]

Best wishes,

Deborah [illegible]

Grappling *with the* GRUMBLIES

Written by Deborah Miller & Illustrated by Diane Jacobs

Grappling with the Grumblies

The illustrations in this book were rendered in pencil and watercolor.
The text was set in 16 point schoolbook.
Book design by Philip Cheaney

Library and Archives Canada Cataloguing in Publication

Miller, Deborah, 1958-
Grappling with the grumblies / Deborah Miller ; illustrations by Diane Jacobs.

ISBN 978-1-897411-09-4

I. Jacobs, Diane (Diane E.), 1966- II. Title.

PS8576.I53646 G73 2009 jC813'.6 C2009-900765-7

First printing: April 2009
Printed in Canada

Books published by Bayeux Arts/Gondolier are available at special quantity discounts to use as premiums and sales promotions, or for use in corporate training programs. For more information, please write to Special Sales, Bayeux Arts, Inc. 119 Stratton Crescent SW, Calgary, Canada T3H1T7.

The publishing activities of Bayeux/Gondolier are supported by the Canada Council for the Arts, the Alberta Foundation for the Arts, and by the Government of Canada through its Book Publishing Industry Development Program.

for
Lizzie, Max and Zusse

One night Mom kissed me good night
and wished me sweet dreams.

I had a good night and sweet dreams.

The next morning Mom woke me up and wished me "Good morning."

I did not have a good morning.

My Mom woke me up too early.

I wanted more sleep.

She turned the light on too fast.

It bugged my eyes.

“Wake up Jessie,”

she said too loudly.

It bugged my ears.

That's when the
Grumblie appeared.

"**GRUMP**," said the Grumblie.

"**GRUMP!**" said I.

And the Grumblie grew.

Mom called, “Breakfast is ready.
Hurry up, please.”

I hate hurrying.

The Grumblie followed me.

We sat grim-faced at the table.

“Toasted bagel and butter with salami, just the way you like it,” Mom said, smiling. “Oh, and don’t forget to drink all your milk.”

"GRUMP! " said the Grumblie.

I said, "Bagels again!" and "I'm sick of milk."

The Grumblie grew.

Mom said, "Stop complaining, and sit properly on your chair."

"GRUMP!" said I.

"GRUMP," said the Grumblie, and the
Grumblie grew and knocked me off my seat.

"Stop messing about and eat!"
Mom said too loudly.
I did not enjoy my breakfast and
I did not drink my milk.
"Get dressed now. We're going to be late,"
Mom said, not smiling.
"GRUMP!" said I.
"GRUMP," said the Grumblie,
and the Grumblie grew.

The Grumblie got up
the stairs before me.

The Grumblie was so big it
got stuck in my doorway.

I had to push and shove
and shove and push just to
get into my own room!

That made me very tired. I had to rest.

Then Mom came in and said,
"Back in bed? Not dressed yet?"

"**GRUMP!**" said I, and the Grumblie grew and fell on my bed.

"Stop that!" I yelled.

"Don't you yell at me!" said Mom.

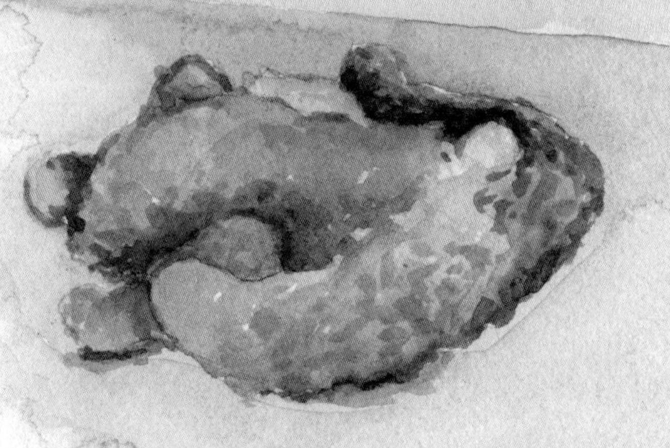

"GRRRRUMP!" said I.
"GRRRRRRUMP!" boomed the Grumblie.
Then the Grumblie grew so big there was no room in my room.

I was stuck!
"I'm, I'm, I'm …
so… Grrrrr!" I said.

My Mom looked straight
into my eyes and said,
"You're grappling with
the Grumblies. Aren't you?"

"Yes," I said.

"I was getting grumpy too," Mom said.

The Grumblie boomed again, but we weren't listening.
"You know, you don't have to grapple with the Grumblie," Mom smiled.
"I don't?" I said.
The Grumblie crossed his arms and tapped his foot.

"C'mon, let's get our Grumblies out!" said Mom and took my hand.
"We'll wiggle those Grumblies away."
We wiggled our hips. We wiggled our toes. We wiggled our fingers.
We wiggled our noses. We wiggled our tummies. We wiggled our bummies.

We looked pretty funny.
We grinned pretty big grins.

"**GRUMP**," the Grumblie said in a small voice.

We grinned from ear to ear
and the Grumblie got smaller.

"Are you still grappling with
the Grumblies?" Mom asked.

"A bit," I said, not in my nicest voice.

"What would you like to do about it?"
Mom asked me.

"I'd like to…shake!"

"Great!" said my Mom.
"We'll shake those Grumblies away!"

We shook our heads.
We shook our hips.
We shook our legs.
We shook our lips!

I shook for having
to wake up early!

Mom shook
for having to rush.

I shook for not
eating my bagel.

Mom shook for
wasted milk.

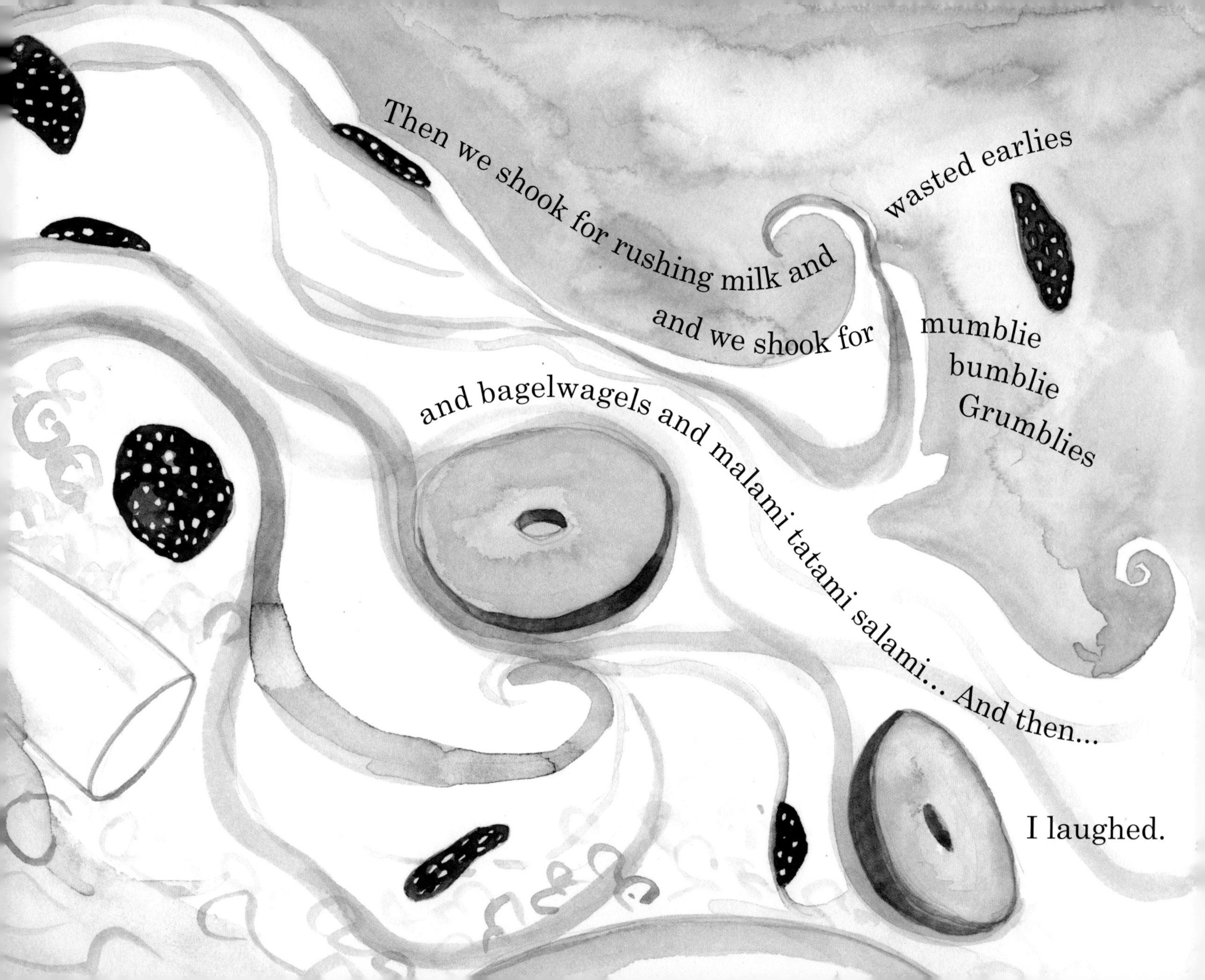
Then we shook for rushing milk and wasted earlies
and we shook for mumblie
bumblie
Grumblies
and bagelwagels and malami tatami salami... And then...
I laughed.

And the Grumblie got smaller.

And then Mom and I both laughed.

And the Grumblie got so small I picked it up and held it in my hand.

And then the Grumblie looked straight into my eyes.

The Grumblie laughed.

“Bye-bye, Grumblie,” I said.

And the Grumblie was gone.

And I went off to school.

Deborah Miller's poetry has been widely published in journals, and her work has been heard on CBC Radio, the Women's Television Network, and Vision TV. Her three poetry collections, *I Will Burn Candles*, *Grandmother's Radio*, co-authored by Susanne Heinz, and *Landing at Night* are published by Bayeux Arts. Deborah lives in Calgary with her husband and daughter. Whenever Deborah grapples with the Grumblies she likes to play Ray Charles songs and dance around the house.

Diane Jacobs received her MFA in printmaking from San Francisco State University in 1996. Her artist books are part of many important collections including The Getty Museum in Los Angeles, The New York Public Library, The San Francisco Museum of Modern Art, The Walker Art Center in Minneapolis, Yale University and Stanford University. Diane lives with her husband and two boys in Portland, Oregon. When Diane grapples with the Grumblies she knows laughter is her best self-defense.

A special thank you to our family and friends for all their support!